We Remember Philip

By Norma Simon

Pictures by Ruth Sanderson

Albert Whitman & Company, Chicago

For David Seidman and Jack Wambach

J
S

Library of Congress Cataloging in Publication Data
Simon, Norma.
    We remember Philip.

    (Concept books)
    Summary: Sam and his classmates seek a way to express
their feelings about the accidental death of their
teacher's son.
    [1. Death—Fiction. 2. Grief—Fiction. 3. School
stories] I. Sanderson, Ruth. II. Title.
PZ7.S6053Wc   [Fic]   78-11691
ISBN 0-8075-8709-5

We Remember Philip

Sam ran over the hill and around the bend in the road to his house. Red faced and hot, even though it was still late winter, he tugged at his book bag.

As he pushed the door open, Rocky, his striped cat, jumped down from the table. Sam picked him up and rocked the big cat in his arms. Rocky purred.

Sam's mother hugged the boy and the cat. She brushed Sam's damp hair back from his face.

"Mom, do you know what happened? My teacher—" Sam stopped and began again. "Mrs. Grout—our principal—was all upset. Mr. Hall didn't come to school. Mom, it's so awful! Mr. Hall's son—he's dead. He was mountain climbing and he fell."

"I know," his mother said. "The news was on the radio and in the paper. Poor, poor Mr. Hall! I feel so sorry for him and his whole family." Tears filled her eyes.

"Oh, Mom, what would you do if . . . if that happened to me?" Sam asked. "If I died?"

His mother spoke gently. "I can't imagine anything more terrible. But you're not going to die. Accidents like this don't happen often. You're going to grow up and have a long, good life. When you're very old, then it will be time to think about the ending."

She pushed his hair back, and Sam knew how much his mother loved him. Now she talked about the Hall family. "There will be long days and nights for them. They'll have to help each other. Suddenly everything is so different from the way it was just yesterday. Oh, Sam, it's so hard!"

Sam put his arms around his mother. "Mom, Mrs. Grout was sad, too, just like you. She cried."

"What did she say, Sam?"

"I don't remember exactly. Everybody was upset. She said Mr. Hall's son, Philip, was climbing with his friends. They were all good climbers. It was an accident. Philip died."

"Did the kids say anything?"

"Nobody knew what to say. Then a substitute came in. She gave us work, but we didn't do much."

Sam's mother sat quietly thinking. Then she said, "Mrs. Grout and everybody who knows Mr. Hall and his family feel their hurt, their grief. We think how we'd feel if this happened to our families. Crying helps when you hurt inside. Men cry, Sam. Your father does sometimes. I hope Mr. Hall lets himself cry."

Sam thought about this, and his mother said, "People wonder what they would do when a death happens. They have to find some way to go on living. That's what the Halls have to do."

"Mom, is there anything I can do? For Mr. Hall, I mean? If you lost me, would anything help you?"

"No, Sam, at first nothing really helps when someone you love dies. Nothing can bring Philip back. But people do need friends, to know others are thinking of them."

"Should I write to him? What if all the kids sent letters?"

Sam's mother smiled at him. "Yes, Mr. Hall needs to know you all care for him. It will help a little later, I think."

Sam let Rocky out. Sitting on the cold doorstep, watching Rocky, Sam began to talk to the big cat just the way he had talked to his old collie dog, Skye.

"Rocky, do you remember Skye? She used to play with you. She watched out for you when you were a kitten. I miss Skye. Do you miss her, Rocky? I cried myself to sleep when she died. We all cried. But Mr. Hall's son—oh, Rocky!"

With a rush of feeling, Sam remembered the night Skye died. He brushed away his tears and stood up. He went inside the house and wrote to Mr. Hall.

A week later, Mr. Hall was staring at his desk as Sam and the other children got off the school bus. They stopped talking at their classroom door. They tiptoed to their desks.

Mr. Hall stood up then and gathered the children around him.

"I'm glad to see you," he said. "It's good to be back. I've missed you. I really have."

Nobody knew what to do or say. The children had never been shy around their teacher, but everything felt different today.

The children looked at each other and back at Mr. Hall. He shook his head, and they saw tears in his eyes. "We don't believe it yet," he said, " . . . that Philip won't be back. Someday you'll understand that it takes a long time to say goodbye. It's like a deep ache. You feel heavy and sick inside. The rest of you stops feeling for a while."

Sam said, "Mr. Hall . . . we're sorry . . . we're all sorry, I mean about Philip and everything. We wanted you to know."

Mr. Hall looked at the girls and boys, and there were still tears in his eyes. He sat down.

"I want to thank you," he said. "Your letters were beautiful. We saved all of them. We needed the love you sent us. We miss our son very much, and talking to you like this, telling you how we feel, having you listen . . . it does help."

But now Mr. Hall stood up. "Work puts the pain aside for a little while. Now let's all get to work. Where are you, Charlie, in your tadpole study? Ben, how's your weather chart? Becky, any sign of spring buds on the trees you're watching? Is your journal up to date, Greg?"

The children squeezed Mr. Hall's hand hard, and some of them gave him a hug, then they went to work. Mr. Hall was brave, they felt, and somehow he and his family would get along.

The winter days passed, one by one. The smiling that once was easy for Mr. Hall was hard. He smiled only when he remembered to and, often, his eyes seemed to look far away. Sometimes he said things like, "I'm sorry, Lisa. I didn't hear that. Will you tell me again, please?"

Sam wished with all his heart that he could help Mr. Hall be his old cheerful, friendly self. On the playground, the children talked about Mr. Hall. "Does he seem better?" they asked each other. "Should we ask about Philip? Does he want to talk about him?"

Slowly, changes came. Mr. Hall laughed again at silly things happening in the classroom. The children smiled at one another and felt glad.

One day, Mr. Hall said, "Emily, when Philip was your age, he had a microscope. He was curious about everything." And this time Mr. Hall did not choke up as he said "Philip."

What gave Sam the idea, he never knew. But one afternoon he said, "Mr. Hall, could you show us pictures of Philip?"

Mr. Hall's face brightened, and his voice was grateful. "Would you like to see some? I'd love to bring in some slides." He gave Sam a special nod. "It's a good idea, Sam. Thanks."

Late on Monday afternoon, Mr. Hall set up the slide projector. Mrs. Grout sat down with the children to watch.

Mr. Hall sounded like any father showing pictures. "Here's Philip and his sister Ruth. They caught those fish . . . This was his first pony ride. He didn't want to stop . . . This picture was taken at camp."

The slides clicked by, and with each click, a new
and older Philip flashed on the screen. The children
watched as Philip grew from a baby to a man.

Mr. Hall's voice was strong and cheerful until the last slide was shown and the screen was blank.

"That's the end. That's all there is," he said.

Mrs. Grout put her hand on Mr. Hall's shoulder. "But it's so much," she told him. "It was a good, happy life. And Philip will stay alive in our memories."

Sam thought about what Mrs. Grout had said. After school, he went to her office. "Won't you miss your bus?" she asked, but he shook his head. "I ride my bike now that the weather is nicer."

"What can I do for you?" she asked in her friendly way.

"Well, you said something to Mr. Hall, and it gave me an idea. You said that when we remember Philip, he stays alive in our memories. Did you mean that?"

"I believe that, don't you?"

"I don't know, Mrs. Grout. I never thought about dying until Philip Hall died."

"Has anyone close to you or your family died?"

"No, I guess I'm lucky. But our old dog Skye died last year. She wasn't a person, but we all cried."

"Do you still remember Skye?"

"Oh, I can still see her all over the place. I still expect her to meet me when I get home."

"So Skye seems to go on the way she used to be just because you remember her that way," said Mrs. Grout. "That's what I meant by staying alive in our memories. But what's your idea, Sam?"

Sam said, "My idea is that maybe it would help Mr. Hall if we could find a special way to remember Philip. What could kids do, Mrs. Grout?"

Mrs. Grout thought, then she said, "Let's do this. Tomorrow Mr. Hall has a meeting at the middle school. I'll be with your class. We can talk together, and I'll try to help you. You know, you people must love Mr. Hall a lot."

"We do. He's the best teacher in this whole school."

The next day when the principal came into their classroom, Charlie asked, "Mrs. Grout, what can we do to help Mr. Hall?"

"You've already done a lot. You've helped him with your letters and by listening to him talk about Philip. There's something else, too. Mr. Hall loves his work. Teaching helps him go on, even when he's lonely for Philip. Yes, I'd say you've already helped him a lot."

Ben asked, "But can we do anything else?"

"What do you want to tell Mr. Hall?"

Ben bit his lip, thinking. Finally he said, "I'm not sure. But we want Mr. Hall to be the way he used to be."

Lisa said, "He seems a little better now, but he doesn't act excited anymore. He acts tired and sad. He's our favorite teacher, but he's not the same as he used to be."

"No, he's not the same," agreed Mrs. Grout. "He'll be more like his old self as time passes and he can remember his son with less pain."

Sam said, "That's the trouble. We want him to remember Philip, but not so that it hurts all the time."

"Can you think of something special you've learned about Philip, something he liked very much?" asked Mrs. Grout.

"He loved the outdoors," Greg said. "And animals," Lisa added.

Sam had a question. "Was Philip tall?"

"Yes," Mrs. Grout answered. "Tall and straight—
like a young tree."

Then Becky asked, "Would a tree be a good way to
remember? Could we plant a tree for Philip?"

All around the room, the children murmured,
"That's right. A tree—that's good."

"An oak tree," Becky said. "An oak tree grows tall
and strong."

"Should we take a vote?" Lisa asked.

"All in favor of an oak tree for Philip, raise your
hand," Sam said.

Twenty hands shot up. And so, with help from Mrs.
Grout, Sam and his friends made plans.

They looked at a tree catalog, and they chose a
special kind of oak, a pin oak. Its leaves would be red
and glossy in the fall.

The children paid for the tree themselves.

Some of the children earned the money by doing chores. Some used their allowances or their treat money.

Mrs. Grout helped them order the tree. They kept it all a secret. "When should we tell Mr. Hall?" Sam asked Mrs. Grout.

"Whenever the class decides. Get some of their ideas," she suggested. "There's plenty of time to talk about it before the tree is delivered."

The cold late winter, when the children had learned the news of Philip's death, slowly changed into an early spring. The wind blew warmer. The earth thawed. Spring rains fell, and the bulbs the children had planted in the school lawn in the fall bloomed.

Mr. Hall was more interested in everything the children were doing.

When the vegetable seed order for the class came in the mail, he was more like himself, excited and eager. Philip used to work in the family garden, he told them. Philip liked to try unusual vegetables with names like Egyptian walking onions, elephant garlic, and vegetable spaghetti.

Sam and the other children noticed that Mr. Hall's voice was steadier now, and it seemed to be easier for him to talk about Philip.

The children shared their secret about the tree with the school custodian, Mr. Dunn. When the tree came, he helped them put it in a safe place.

"A fine tree," he said.

Now, the children decided, it was time to tell Mr. Hall, and they chose Becky to speak for everyone.

"Mr. Hall," she began, "we decided—Mrs. Grout helped us—that we want to do something. Something special. We want to plant an oak tree . . . it will be Philip's tree. To remember him, you see. Will you help us plant it?"

Mr. Hall's face showed his surprise, a mixture of being happy and sad at the same time. He listened to the plans.

"I'll be glad to help," he said. "I think you can tell how deeply I feel. A tree is a beautiful way to remember our son Philip."

Greg said, "Even if we never knew him, we miss Philip. Do you know what we mean?"

"Yes," Mr. Hall answered. "Before, Philip was just part of my family and his friends. Now he's part of your lives, too. He'd like that—being part of such good people."

*I*t was a beautiful day for the tree planting.

The Hall family, Mrs. Grout, and all the children in Sam's class gathered on the green school lawn.

Mr. Dunn had helped the children carry the tree to its place. He had a spade ready for digging. In his wheelbarrow was peat moss to mix with the soil.

Mr. Dunn, Sam, and the other children, Mr. Hall, and Kate and Ruth, Philip's sisters, all took turns digging. Mrs. Hall held the tree, its roots wrapped in burlap, and the children pushed the warm soil around it.

Every little while, Mr. Dunn would say, "Stamp on the earth with one foot. Good!"

At the end, the children patted down the last of the rich topsoil with their hands. They left a ring of soil around the tree, like a big saucer, to hold the water it would need to grow.

"Philip would have liked the way you people work," Mr. Hall told them. "It's a strong young tree in good soil."

"I'll put in a pole later," Mr. Dunn said. "Can't let the wind shake it too hard while it's young. Charlie, hook up the hose to water the tree. Come on Becky, help us."

A few children carried Mr. Dunn's tools and pushed the wheelbarrow back to the school basement. The rest sat down on the grass, tired and quiet, their shoes and hands still brown with earth. The Halls sat down with them, and soon the other children returned.

Sam's eyes moved from the fresh dark soil around the tree trunk to his teacher. He wondered what Mr. Hall was thinking. As if he heard Sam's thoughts, Mr. Hall said, "That was good, helping you plant Philip's tree."

Becky touched the thin tree trunk. "Someday, you'll be thirty feet tall," she said.

Mrs. Hall and Kate and Ruth moved closer to Mr. Hall. Mrs. Hall took his hand in hers. She looked at him and smiled as he started to speak to Sam and all the others.

"You've given me the strength," he said, "to go on from day to day. I'll watch this oak tree grow, and I'll remember Philip. And I'll remember each of you and how you shared and eased my pain. You've helped me say my goodbye to Philip."

Thoughts on Talking with Children About Death

Children often feel personally threatened when death touches their lives, even a death in another family. They need time to talk about their concern for their own lives and the lives of people whom they love. They need assurance that most people do live long lives.

Death is a painful subject for many adults, and as a result, it is a topic usually avoided in discussions with children. But children are more capable of understanding and responding to the meanings of death than is generally supposed. The experience of death need not be burdened with mystery, fear, and secrecy which so commonly disturb children.

Children have a tremendous capacity for sympathy and for reaching out to others. Given the chance, they can learn to be patient and comforting with someone who is recovering from a deep loss. In times of trouble, children have strengths to share that can help make grief bearable. But girls and boys need the opportunity to have their concern and help accepted by adults.

Memories of people whom we have loved and who have died often help secure our own living and loving in the present. The importance we place on these recollections can help our children deal with their own future experiences.

In a lifetime, each of us knows much heartfelt joy and sadness as we love and care for those close to us. Children become more caring adults if they, too, share in the joy and sorrow that are important parts of living and maturing.

NORMA SIMON